ROSCO THE RASCAL
IN THE
LAND OF SNOW

Rosco the Rascal #2

By Shana Gorian

Illustrations by Ros Webb

Cover Art by Josh Addessi & Tori March

Rosco the Rascal in the Land of Snow.
Copyright © 2015 by Shana Gorian. All Rights Reserved.

Cover Art by Josh Addessi & Tori March.
Illustrations by Ros Webb.
Cover design by Kim Killion.

All rights reserved under International and Pan American Copyright conventions. No part of this book may be reproduced, transmitted, downloaded, recorded, or stored in any information storage and retrieval system, in any form or by any means, whether electronic or mechanical, now known or hereinafter invented, without the express written permission of the publisher, except for brief quotations for review purposes.

This is a work of fiction. Names, characters, places, and incidents are products of the author's imagination or are used fictitiously and are not to be construed as real. Any resemblance to actual events, locales, organizations, or persons, living or dead, is entirely coincidental.

First Edition, 2015

Oh! The snow, the beautiful snow,
Filling the sky and earth below,
Over the housetops, over the street,
Over the heads of the people you meet.

~Thomas J. Watson

CONTENTS

CHAPTER 1

WHAT'S THAT?

Rosco peered out the side window, wondering if they were finally here. Mandy opened the door to the minivan, and Rosco, the family dog, jumped out. His paws sunk down into the cold, white snow. Where were they? Wow, it was cold!

At long last, the drive was over. The McKendricks had arrived at the winter cabin, in all of its snowy glory. The kids climbed carefully out of the van and into the frosty air.

"This looks like the exact opposite of where we live," seven-year-old Mandy whispered in amazement.

Rosco thought so, too.

Dad began unloading the luggage. Mom stepped out and stretched her legs, admiring the cabin and yard. Mandy's ten-year-old brother, James, gazed up at the enormous snow-covered pine trees in awe.

Quickly, Rosco, the large German shepherd, decided that he liked this place and the fluffy stuff that his family called *snow*. This could be fun! He licked it. Very refreshing!

Just then, something rustled in the bushes beside the cabin. Rosco's ears perked up. What was that? He darted toward the snow-covered bushes to investigate.

"Uh-oh," said Mandy to her parents with dismay. "Rosco found something already. What do you think is in there?"

Rosco sniffed at the bushes. He heard a small whimper, then, more rustling in the low branches.

Three noisy squirrels scampered out of the bushes. Snow showered from their branches. The squirrels raced across the ground and up the nearest pine tree. One of them carried an acorn in its mouth.

"Oh, it's just a few squirrels," Dad said. He turned back to the luggage. "Come on, kids, grab a suitcase."

But Rosco wasn't convinced. He knew he had heard more than just a few squirrels. He waited for the sound again, but all was silent in the bushes.

"Come on, Rosco," James called. "Let's go see the cabin!"

Rosco turned away from the bushes and the squirrels, obeying his owner like a good dog. The noise could wait. He was excited to see the cabin, too.

He followed the family up the wooden staircase and across the porch. James and Mandy kicked the snow off of their boots.

"Wow! It's so nice!" Mom exclaimed as they entered the house. She shut the door tightly behind them.

Meanwhile, just outside the door, the bushes rustled again. More snow scattered to the ground. A small, four-legged creature stuck its furry head out from under a bush. It glanced about, carefully checking that no one had caught a glimpse of its soft, brownish white fur.

No one had. Quickly, the creature bolted for the forest behind the cabin and was gone.

CHAPTER 2
CABIN IN THE WOODS

Earlier that afternoon, on the drive to the cabin, James leaned forward anxiously. "How much longer until we get there, Dad?" he asked.

"About two more hours," Dad said.

"Aw, man. We've only been driving for an hour? It seems like much longer than that," he said, and slouched back in his seat.

It was a chilly Friday afternoon in February. The McKendrick family was headed for the mountains. They drove up narrow, winding, mountain roads on their way to a log cabin deep in the woods.

Mr. and Mrs. McKendrick had rented the

two-bedroom cabin for the weekend. The family usually visited the mountains once each winter, either for just one day to go sledding, or sometimes, for a whole weekend. But, they had never rented *this* cabin before. So it would be a new adventure for all of them.

The rental agency said that it had a big front yard and a large, stone fireplace. Dad brought along a bundle of firewood in case the cabin wasn't stocked.

"There's supposed to be a good sledding hill that's only a short walk from our cabin," said Dad. "They said you can almost see it from the cabin."

"I can't wait to go sledding!" Mandy shrieked with delight.

James, a fifth grader with red hair and freckles, and Mandy, a second grader with long, straight, brown hair, sat buckled in the backseat, watching the beautiful winter scenery go by.

Rosco sat on the floor of the minivan,

looking out of the window too.

Rosco had never seen snow before. He watched in wonder as they passed rocks, pine trees, and cabins covered in mounds of fluffy, white powder.

Rosco was only two years old. He was a big dog, weighing eighty-five pounds. His fur was mostly black, but he had tan legs and a little bit of white fur that highlighted his face and paws.

He was playful and full of energy, and had a terribly loud and frightening bark. So Mandy and James always felt safe with Rosco around.

Rosco had become such a trusted member of the family that he now went nearly everywhere they did, even on weekend trips.

The cabin where they'd be staying was nestled in the mountains, in a thick pine forest. It was far from the suburbs where the McKendricks lived. It was at such a high

elevation that there was always snow on the ground in winter.

That's why the family went to the mountains, because at their house, they didn't get much snow. Some years they didn't get any at all.

Once in a while it would get really cold, and maybe an inch or two would fall. But most of the time in winter, they would just get rain: boring, old rain. You couldn't ride sleds on rain and you couldn't build a snowman out of rain.

So if they wanted to play in the snow, they had to take a trip to the snow. That's where the long drive and the cabin came in.

And yes, the drive *was* long, but it was also exciting. To get to the cabin, they had to follow a long, curving road, high into the mountains.

"Wow! Look at that drop-off, kids!" Dad said as he drove. Mandy looked out the window and squealed with fright.

The sky had become foggy, and the snow was falling. Dad had begun to drive very slowly.

"I can't look," James said, putting one hand over his queasy stomach and the other over his mouth.

Even though salt trucks and snowplows were working hard to keep the road as clear as possible, a flashing yellow sign appeared on the roadside ahead. It warned that chains were required for all vehicles continuing on, because the roads might get slippery. A little further down the road, a police officer stood waiting to stop travelers and check that they had obeyed the sign.

Chains were like steel nets that fastened onto a car's tires. They kept the car from slipping and sliding all over the road.

Dad cautiously pulled the car to the side of the road and parked.

"It's time," Dad said.

He pulled on his winter hat and stepped out into the snow. He opened the rear door, and dug out the chains from the trunk. Mom climbed into the driver's seat after she rolled down her front window.

Dad dropped to his knees and rolled out one set of chains behind each front tire. He stepped back from the van.

"Back it up!" he called to Mom. "Just a tad." Mom slowly moved the van in reverse.

"Stop there!" Dad called. "Looking good."

The front tires were now sitting directly on top of the chains. Dad grabbed the ends of each set and wrapped them around the tires, latching them in place.

"Okay honey, time to test them. Drive forward now!" he instructed. "But very slowly."

James and Mandy held their breath. Mom drove forward just a few inches.

"Perfect!" Dad said. "They're as snug as can be."

"Whew," James said. "Done."

Behind them, car after car lined up along the side of the road, as drivers secured their chains.

"We're all set!" Dad said as he sat back down in the car. His knees were soaked from the snow.

"Dad, your hands are filthy now! Why are they so dirty?" Mandy said, astonished. Mom handed Dad a wet wipe and settled back into her seat on the passenger's side.

"That's from the dirty grime all over the tires. My hands are freezing cold now, too! That's *not* a job you can do wearing gloves!"

Mom cranked up the heater as Dad wiped his hands clean.

"This drive will be a cinch, now," Dad said, turning the windshield wipers back on.

He pulled the car back onto the snowy, white road. "But it will take a while!"

The minivan inched forward, slowly but surely.

CHAPTER 3

A BLIZZARD?

That night, after the long drive, the sun went down shortly after they arrived at the cabin. The temperature dropped below freezing. The snow continued to fall.

James and Mandy wanted to play outside. But the snow was falling too hard.

"It must be a blizzard!" James declared, looking out at the black sky dotted with millions of white snowflakes. "Like the ones we read about in science class last month!"

Then he corrected himself. "Well, actually, it's probably just a snow storm. The wind isn't blowing hard enough to be a true blizzard."

Still, they weren't able to play outside that evening. The snow was falling so hard that they couldn't see more than a few feet in front of their faces. The kids were very disappointed.

"Don't worry. The snow will be there in the morning, kids," Dad said.

So, Mandy and James played the board games from the cabin's closets, instead. They watched a movie on TV. Dad built a roaring fire in the fireplace. Mom made hot cocoa with marshmallows. Things turned out just fine.

The fantastic snowstorm continued throughout the night, creating a whole new layer of fresh snow.

CHAPTER 4

ALL THAT SNOW

Saturday morning arrived, and the kids were up early. But it was still dark outside. James and Mandy squinted, trying to peer through the fogged-up glass of the large window in their room.

Mandy wiped the frosty windowpane in circles with the edge of her sleeve. She was trying to clear a spot so that they could see into the backyard.

"Look at all that snow," she sighed. "Everything's completely covered in it. It's just so perfect."

But now her sleeve was wet and cold. She shivered.

"Can you believe it? It's still coming down," said James in a whisper. "I can't wait to get out there. I wonder how many inches of snow fell overnight?"

Just then, Rosco slinked up the spiral wooden staircase and trotted over.

The kids' bedroom was in an open loft on the second floor, above the living room. There was a spiral staircase to get to it. The loft had walls on only three sides. On the fourth side, there was a half wall, with a wooden banister that you could look over, down into the living room below.

There you'd see the old, stone fireplace, the comfortable sofa, and the charming front door. The loft had a set of bunk beds, with a wooden ladder so that you could climb to the top bunk.

Mom and Dad didn't need to come up here at all. It was the kids' very own space.

Rosco squeezed his furry head between the kids so that he could look out of the window, too. He gazed at the snowy scene, panting and wearing his famous doggy grin.

But then he noticed some movement in the snow. "Ruff! Ruff! Ruff!" he barked. Immediately his breath fogged up the clear spot on the window.

"Shh!" said the kids. "You'll wake up

Mom and Dad. We're not allowed to make noise until seven o'clock." They hadn't seen any movement outside.

So Rosco began to lick the window instead. He wanted to clear another spot through which to see.

"Don't lick it, Rosco! That won't work. It'll just fog up again," Mandy laughed.

"And your tongue might stick," James said.

"Maybe Rosco's thirsty if he's licking the frost off of the window?" said James.

He called quietly for Rosco to follow him to the kitchen. He'd go get the dog some water and take him outside to do his morning business.

"Quiet, boy," he said. Quickly, he dug out a measuring tape from his suitcase. "I packed this so I could measure how much snow is on the ground. I'm going to measure it right now."

Mandy nodded. "Oh, cool!"

James and Rosco carefully tiptoed down

the narrow stairs and out the kitchen door. Mandy stayed by the window, watching the falling snow. She thought it was strange that Rosco would bark for no reason.

Suddenly, Mandy noticed a tiny, four-legged creature standing at the edge of the yard, gazing up at the warm cabin. Mandy squinted again, trying to see more clearly. "What's that?" she said in surprise. "It looks like a puppy!"

She covered her mouth to prevent another outburst. What would a puppy be doing out there in the dark and in the snow? Mandy began to worry.

She watched as James bent down and pushed the measuring tape straight into the snow. He did not see the small creature in the low light of the early morning. But he watched as Rosco raced across the backyard in the animal's direction. Rosco's powerful nose had told him exactly where it was.

The creature was too quick, however. In a flash, it turned and disappeared into the woods.

Mandy desperately scanned the trees as she peered out the window, but it was useless. The animal was gone.

Rosco scared it off! Why was it afraid of Rosco? He wouldn't hurt a puppy. That's strange. Maybe it's lost. What if it lives in one of the other cabins down the road?

Mandy glanced at the clock on the wall. It read five minutes to seven. How long would it take for Mom and Dad to wake up?

Outside, James pulled his measuring tape out of the snow. He called to Rosco. "Come back, boy!"

Rosco heard James call him, so he turned around and headed back toward the house. He'd find that animal later. He had caught a whiff of the animal's scent and knew that it was a young, male creature very similar to Rosco, himself. But Rosco hadn't gotten a good look at him. Why had he run from him?

CHAPTER 5
BACON AND WAFFLES

"Mandy! Breakfast is almost ready!" Mom called from the kitchen. The delicious smells of bacon and maple syrup were just starting to fill the tiny cabin.

Mom was already up? Mandy raced down the spiral stairs and headed for the kitchen. She inhaled deeply.

"Mmm...bacon!"

The kitchen door swung open with a blast of Arctic air. James trudged in from the backyard, kicking snow off his boots.

"It's *still* coming down out there!" he said. "But not as fast as it was last night." His sweater was dotted with wet snowflakes.

"There are almost two feet of snow on the ground! At least that's as deep as I could get the measuring tape to go. Probably six inches of fresh powder fell overnight!"

James took off his boots and placed them on the doormat. His red hair was covered in tiny speckles of snow. He opened the back door again and called for Rosco to come in.

"Are the waffles ready yet, Mom?" James asked. "I'm starving."

"Yes, they are," she replied. "But wash your hands first, honey."

Rosco trotted up the stairs of the back porch and into the warm room. He shook out his wet fur, sending snow sailing onto the kitchen floor. It melted quickly as he sauntered over to inspect his bowl. He began to devour the dog food as if he hadn't eaten in weeks.

This cold weather sure gives me a big appetite! Rosco thought. Was the pup hungry too?

"This fresh powder is the best kind for

making snowballs. Did you know that?" James asked his mother. She nodded. He was always full of useful facts.

"Oh yeah, I meant to tell you, Rosco thought he saw something out there," James added. "He took off after it, but he came right back when I called him. I couldn't see what he was chasing. Must've been nothing."

"Well, you kids should be careful out there. Wild animals live in these woods. We're in their territory, after all," Mom said.

James looked surprised. Mandy was concerned. "*Wild* animals?"

"Oh, don't worry, honey. Just keep your eyes wide open, and be aware of what's around you," Mom cautioned. "And James, you know all about animals from the books you read and the nature shows you watch on TV. I'm surprised you hadn't realized that they could be here. I didn't mean to scare you guys," she said gently.

James did know that. He had read the list of animals that lived in these mountains when Dad researched the cabin on the Internet. There were rabbits, squirrels, foxes, raccoons, owls, hawks, deer, bobcats, coyotes, and even mountain lions and black bears.

"I saw what he was chasing. It looked like a little puppy," said Mandy.

"Really?" James and his mother both answered in surprise.

"Well, I'm not totally *sure* it was a puppy. It was hard to tell. But I know it had four legs and it was small," Mandy added. "Maybe it was a little fox?"

"I'm sure it's nothing to worry about. Plus, you know what a good guard dog Rosco is," Mom said. "He's always on the lookout. Don't be afraid."

James relaxed. He was planning on plenty of outdoor activities this weekend. For instance, having a snowball fight, sledding, and building a snowman.

James also planned to try Rosco out as a sled dog, like a Siberian husky in Alaska. He was sure his powerful dog would be able to pull them on a sled. He hadn't told Mandy about his idea. It was a surprise, but he was sure she would love the ride.

James did not want to let the thought of wild and ferocious beasts ruin all of that.

He'd stick to his winter fun to-do list for the weekend, as planned. He'd just be aware of his surroundings, as his mother had advised.

After all, in all of the years that they had been coming to the mountains in the winter, they had never before seen anything more than rabbits and deer. Those other animals stayed as far away from humans as possible.

"Take this to your father and wake him up," Mom said, handing Mandy a cup of steaming, hot coffee with cream. "Tell him hibernation is only for the bears."

Bears would be hibernating this time of year anyway, James realized. No need to worry about *them*, at least. He sighed in relief.

Mandy opened the door to her parents'

bedroom.

"Hi, Dad! Mom told me to wake you up." She carefully set the coffee cup on the nightstand.

Dad lifted his ruffled head for a moment to look at her through one eye. He rolled over and pulled a pillow over his head. "In a minute." He yawned, and quickly went back to sleep.

"Mom made waffles," Mandy whispered.

No reply came from Dad. Mandy shook her head and sighed.

All month Mandy had looked forward to this trip. She had marked an X on her calendar every day as the weeks passed, crossing her fingers and wishing that time would just *go by faster*!

So here they were, and she was ready. She wanted to play in the snow, and see if Rosco loved the snow as much as she did. Dad would have to catch up later. Her waffles were waiting. And so was all of that snow!

CHAPTER 6

SNOW DOG

An hour later, Mr. McKendrick came out of the bedroom, rubbing his eyes.

"Anything left to eat?" he asked cheerfully, as he poured himself a second cup from the coffee pot.

A plate of cold food sat on the counter for him. He covered it with a paper towel, set it inside the microwave oven, and pressed the start button.

Mom was just finishing up the dishes. James and Mandy were practicing Rosco's lineup of tricks with him. Both kids had finished breakfast, made their beds, and helped Mom clean up the kitchen.

"Roll over, that's right! Over!" James said. Rosco rolled and then sat up again.

"Now, give the paw." Rosco held up his paw to shake.

"Are you kids going to get dressed for the outdoors soon? It looks like the snow has finally slowed down out there," Mom said. "The snow clothes are hanging by the front door."

"Yeah! Let's go!" James said.

James grabbed his boots and mittens from the kitchen doormat, since he had already used them this morning.

The kids pulled their bulky snow pants and rubber boots over their jeans and socks.

Mandy grabbed her red coat. Her cap was pink, and had a pom-pom on top. It had braided ties that dangled below her ears like extra ponytails over her long hair.

James's coat was blue, with black pockets and zippers. It matched the blue and gray beanie he wore on his head.

It was a lot of work dressing for the snow.

When the kids were younger and needed help, Mom often used the word *exhausting* to describe the process. But at long last, today the kids were bundled up and ready for the cold weather with no help at all.

Outside, the snow had finally stopped falling. Everything in sight was pure, whitewashed magic.

"I've got two extra pieces of bacon left. Who wants them?" Mom called.

"I do!" James said as he trudged back into the kitchen in his snow gear.

Mandy stepped cautiously out the front door into the dreamlike world alone. It was peaceful and quiet. She gazed up at the pale, white sky. The thermometer outside the cabin's door read twenty-nine degrees Fahrenheit—cold but not *too* cold.

Mandy wasted no time. She carefully hopped down the slippery porch stairs, one at a time, holding onto the porch banister.

She looked around, just as Mom had instructed, to be sure she wasn't surprising any wild animals that might be passing by.

Nope, nothing. Not even a deer. Good.

She plopped down in the yard and flailed her arms and legs from side to side to make her first snow angel of the season.

Carefully, she pulled herself to her feet to admire her work. It was magnificent.

But she hadn't closed the front door tightly. Rosco pushed his way through and came bounding out into the yard, sending snow flying off the ground in every direction.

"Ruff, ruff!" he barked.

"Hey, boy! I was just going to call for you! It's time to play!" she said.

Rosco raced up to Mandy, leaving his paw prints all over her snow angel. *Let's play! Let's play!*

Mandy's perfect snow angel was now a perfect mess.

"Rosco! Watch where you're going!" she scolded.

Mandy had been so eager to see her dog play in the snow that she decided not to let it bother her. She quickly set to work on another angel, stretching out on the ground.

This time, Rosco decided to try it, too. He lay down in the snow next to her and rolled over, stretching and turning with funny jerking motions.

Mandy sat up and looked at him,

laughing. "You're making a snow angel too, Rosco! Aren't you? Good boy!" She studied Rosco's snow angel. "Actually, it doesn't really look like one. But after all, you're just a dog. I'll call it a snow dog!"

Rosco's good behavior didn't last long. He lifted his hind leg over his snow dog. A deep yellow puddle began clouding up the white snow.

"Oh Rosco! What are you doing? Yuck! It's totally ruined now! You are impossible!" Mandy clenched both fists.

She didn't want to be mad at Rosco, so she took a deep breath and calmed down.

"Okay. Well, let's try something else." Rosco wagged his tail in agreement.

James appeared on the porch. He marched down the stairs and across the yard, sinking down into the snow with each step. His snow pants made swishing noises as he walked.

Mom stuck her head out the door. "Are you guys going to build a snowman?"

"Yes!" said Mandy. "Especially since Rosco is destroying every snow angel I make. But, look! He also made one by himself, and look what he did to it!"

Mom saw the yellow snow and wrinkled her nose. "Oh boy, that rascal. Rosco, what are we going to do with you?" Rosco just wagged his tail eagerly at Mom and panted.

"Did he at least wait until you got up off the ground, Mandy?" James said, nearly falling over with laughter. "Rosco, dogs are supposed to use trees for that, you know!"

"I'll go get the carrot I brought for the snowman's nose," Mom said, giving James a stern look as she turned and headed into the house.

CHAPTER 7

TUG-OF-WAR

James picked up some snow from the ground and packed it into the shape of a snowball. Then he set it on the ground and began to roll it around the yard. With each roll, the snowball grew larger and larger.

Meanwhile, Rosco inspected the yard, looking for traces of the pup's scent. He sniffed at the walls of the cabin. He sniffed at the pile of firewood on the porch. He sniffed at the base of each nearby tree and rock.

Mandy began searching for sticks and rocks for the snowman's arms and face, but something else in the snow caught her eye.

"Oh wow, look at these tracks!" She knelt

down for a closer look.

They were a lot like Rosco's tracks, just smaller. And this was the spot where she saw the animal from the window! It had to be a dog. It just had to.

She followed the tracks to the edge of the woods. They continued into the forest.

Mandy wouldn't go in there alone. She strained her eyes to see into the forest. But the pup was gone.

"Rosco, come!" she called. "Look what I found!"

Rosco bounded over. Mandy had found more of the puppy's scent! The pup had been all over this yard. Rosco wagged his tail with excitement, sniffing around.

"We have to wait until he comes back out of the woods. Don't go in there, boy."

Out front, Mom reappeared on the porch. "That looks like a good place to put the snowman, James," Mom said.

She watched her son roll the snowball into place, right smack dab in the center of the yard. It had grown very large, so James was now struggling to move it. He finished one last heavy turn and let the giant snowball rest where it stopped.

"Whew! Yep, this'll do," he agreed. "I almost broke a sweat! In *this* weather!"

Mom smiled and set the carrot down on the snow-covered porch railing. "I'll leave it right here, then." She went back inside. James quickly went back to work.

Mandy returned from her backyard hunt

with Rosco and dropped a handful of small, odd-shaped rocks into the snow. She laid two long, skinny sticks down next to them and told James about the tracks.

Rosco sniffed at her findings and snatched up one of the sticks.

"Rosco, those are for the snowman!" Mandy tried to take the stick from him.

But this rascal of a dog wanted to play. He began shaking his head back and forth with such force that Mandy could barely hold on. She quickly let go.

Rosco didn't mind. He was done with their game of tug-of-war just as quickly as he had started it. He nestled down in the snow. Ferociously, he began chewing on the stick.

"Rosco, I looked all over the place to find that stick. And you're going to rip it apart now, aren't you?"

"Mandy, can you come and help me put the middle piece on the snowman?" said her brother.

Rosco continued to chew on the stick.

"Sure." Mandy plodded over to help.

CHAPTER 8

A HUFF AND A HOWL

"Wow. You work fast, James," said Mandy.

The snowball that James had rolled into place was almost three feet wide. But it wasn't completely round.

James had also made a second snowball. It wasn't perfect either.

"One, two, three—roll!" James instructed Mandy. "Steady. Don't let go!"

They rolled. The second snowball settled into place. Some snow fell off, but most of it stayed together.

"Well, I guess it could be worse," James said. They packed on more snow to round it out.

Mandy studied the snowman, still a little unsure. It looked like a white boulder with a big, white lump on top.

"Hmmm," she said. It wasn't so great yet.

Suddenly, Rosco looked up from his chewing and dropped his stick. He jumped to his feet and stood to listen.

High-pitched yelping came from the trees. *"Ee-oo-ee-oo-ee-oo."* It sounded like a baby animal crying for attention.

Then, an eerie, high-pitched howl followed. It sounded much farther off and was from the other direction.

"Ow-ow-ow-oooooo!"

Mandy froze in place. "What was *that*?" All of a sudden, she was scared. "Where'd it come from?"

He pointed at the forest behind the cabin. "Over there," said James. "It sounded like a coyote, didn't it?"

"Yeah, but what was that first noise?" she asked.

"I have no idea," James said.

Not wasting a moment, Rosco ran for the woods. He just *had* to investigate. If something dangerous were lurking in the forest, he would make sure it stayed away.

"Rosco, wait!" Mandy called urgently. But the dog did not stop.

"Uh-oh. Okay, let's not panic. He'll chase it off, whatever it was," said James.

They often heard coyote howls from the hills surrounding their home in the suburbs, so James, Mandy, and Rosco were no strangers to those sounds.

Plus, Rosco was much bigger than a coyote, and almost twice as heavy as most of them. He would not likely be in danger, as long as there wasn't a whole pack. Still, the kids worried.

"That's odd they're still howling in the daytime," James said. "Coyotes should be back in their dens by now."

Half a minute passed as they watched to see if anything would come out of the woods. Nothing did. It grew very quiet.

"I'm scared," said Mandy. "But I don't want to go in the house until Rosco comes back. Let's wait here until he does."

"Well, okay. But let's wait on the porch," James said.

Mandy agreed. They turned to head toward the cabin.

Just then, Dad stepped out of the front door, dressed for the snow. He was holding a red shovel and a brown scarf. He gazed sadly at the long driveway and their snowed-in van.

"Wow-eeee! It's chilly out here! I'd better wear my gloves." He walked down the stairs, leaned the shovel against the house and reached into his pockets to pull out his gloves.

"Where's Rosco?" he asked, squeezing his hands into them.

James and Mandy explained.

"Hmm," Dad said. "Well, coyotes do live out here. But they generally avoid people and will only attack if they feel threatened or if they're protecting their young. So, don't worry. They won't bother you."

Just then Rosco skipped out of the woods.

"Rosco! You're back!" said the kids with relief. Rosco looked as healthy and happy as ever. He was unhurt and thrilled from the chase. He wished that he could tell his people what he had seen.

Mandy ran to him and hugged him around the neck. "Oh, thank goodness you're okay!"

He had indeed seen a coyote. She was a full-grown female with a thick, tan and white coat and a bushier tail than his. Smaller than he was and well camouflaged, her thick fur and light colors blended in well with the snow.

But as soon as he had come upon her, she'd bolted away, deeper into the forest.

"We were starting to worry, Rosco," Mandy said. "I wonder what you saw in there."

Rosco panted and sat down on the snow

to rest.

"Whatever it is, it's gone now," said James.

"That's right. It's gone. Don't let this spoil your fun, guys," said Dad. "Sometimes coyotes are still wandering about during the daylight hours, getting back to their dens. They howl to locate one another sometimes. It's no big deal if you just keep your wits about you and keep this strong, protective, dog close. Now, on to what *is* a big deal— shoveling that snow-covered driveway. I'd better get to work."

Then Dad said, "Oh, before I forget, Here's the scarf. Mom said you'd be needing it."

Finally, he noticed the snowman. "So, there it is," he said. "Your snowman is almost done."

"Well, sort of," said James. "Come see it."

CHAPTER 9

THE SNOWMAN

Dad grabbed the shovel and walked out into the yard with James and Mandy. He laid it on the ground. Then he draped the brown wool scarf around the two lumps of snow, crossing one end over the other in the front.

"There you go," Dad said. "Lookin' good!"

Now the snowman was a white boulder with a white lump on top and a silly brown ribbon across the middle.

"Wait, Dad, we haven't made the head yet," said James. "You just wrapped the scarf around its waist."

Mandy laughed. "Looks like more of a belt."

"Oh, I see. Okay, then," said Dad. He removed the scarf and set it on the ground. James set to work packing one more snowball for the head.

"I'm going to go find another stick," said Mandy. "Come on, Rosco! Let's go for a walk!"

"Did you bring the hat, Dad?" James asked.

"Oops! I forgot. I wonder where it is," said Dad. "Your mother will know. She asked me to bring both. I'll go get it." He sighed and trudged back to the cabin.

In a little while, Mandy and Rosco returned with more sticks. She dropped one for Rosco.

"You can have this one so you'll leave mine alone!" she said.

Rosco lay back down on the snow and began chewing away at the new, delicious stick.

"Success!" said James, stepping away from his work. Three snowballs finally sat in place, one on top of the other, stable and strong. The result was only slightly crooked.

"It's not half bad!" said Mandy. She positioned her rocks on the snowman's face: two eyes and a smile. She had enough left over to place two buttons down his middle.

James walked to the porch and grabbed the carrot. "And now for the centerpiece," he said as he stuck it into the snowman's face. He twisted the carrot so it would stay put as the snowman's nose.

He picked up the scarf from the ground and carefully wrapped it around the snowman's neck.

"It's looking really good now, if you ask me," James said proudly.

"We still need the hat," Mandy realized. "I wonder if Dad found it by now."

"He probably did. Let's go get Mom and Dad so we can show them, now that it's finished." Mandy and James headed for the house.

Rosco watched them leave. Where were

they going? He had not been paying any attention to the kids as he chewed the stick into a million pieces.

His eyes rested on the snowman. Wow, they finished their snow person? What was that on its face? Food? He sniffed the air and headed toward the snowman.

Rosco always wanted food. Dog food was great. But people food—hot dogs, mashed potatoes, steak, and almost any table scrap, for that matter —was something he was willing to try. He was not a picky dog.

When he reached the snowman, he circled it, sniffing it all over.

The snowman was at least as tall as James. Rosco perched on his hind legs, stretching up to inspect its face. He dug his paws into the snowman's middle to keep his balance. Some snow fell off.

He sniffed the snowman's head and licked it. He made so many paw print holes on the snowman's middle that it started to look like a piece of Swiss cheese.

Rosco knew the man was made of snow. But there was definitely food on his face. Now why would that be there? They never leave food sitting around outside, unless it was for him?

He gazed at the carrot, wondering. He looked the snowman directly in the eyes and decided to test the carrot. Maybe they were being thoughtful, and left him a treat?

He had never tasted a carrot before. He

carefully plucked it from the snowman's face, held it in his sharp teeth, and sank back down on all four legs.

He crunched. Yum! The large carrot broke in half. Rosco held onto one piece and let the other fall to the ground.

Just then, the small creature Rosco had chased into the woods that morning ran out from the trees, straight toward Rosco. It was the pup! It stopped a few feet away, licking its lips and whining softly.

Rosco quickly realized that it wasn't the same kind of dog that he was. It was a coyote

puppy!

The coyote he saw in the woods must be its mother! She's looking for him! That's why she was here!

The pup whimpered. He was unsure if this big dog was friendly, but he was ready to find out, since Rosco looked a little like a coyote, after all.

Rosco thought the pup must be hungry. He pushed the remaining piece of carrot to the pup's front paws. The coyote pup was very hungry, indeed. He quickly devoured what was left of the carrot. Now only tiny, orange slivers remained on the clean, white snow.

Thanks, the puppy yipped.

Rosco smiled and wagged his tail. Poor kid. He must be lost.

The next moment, the front door to the cabin creaked. Someone was coming out of the house. But before anyone stepped onto the porch, the coyote pup dashed off into the woods. None of the family saw him.

Only Rosco turned and watched him run away. Rosco barked. *Come back! They won't hurt you!*

But the coyote pup was gone.

CHAPTER 10

GUILTY PARTY

Mom and Dad followed the kids to the yard. It was time for an official snowman viewing.

Rosco ran up to Mandy, dancing about, eager to let her know that the pup had just been there. But he didn't know how he could make her understand. She was already so excited about the snowman.

Mandy skipped ahead and was the first to reach the front of the snowman, which was facing away from the house.

"Oh no! You've got to be kidding me!" Mandy exclaimed, startled.

"What in the world?" said Mom, hurrying over to find out what had happened.

"The carrot's missing!" Mandy said.

Rosco raised his ears. Wasn't that carrot meant for him?

Mom looked at Rosco, then back at the snowman and Mandy's now angry frown. They both saw the doggie paw prints on the snowman's midsection and all over the ground. Mom noticed the traces of orange in the snow. It didn't take her long to figure out what Mandy had quickly realized.

Dad and James reached the front of the snowman just as Mom stooped down to search the ground for evidence.

"What happened? The snowman's a mess!" James said. "And where's the carrot?"

In her most serious voice, Mom spoke very slowly to the dog. "Rosco, what—did—you—do?" She stared into Rosco's eyes.

The dog suddenly felt very guilty, although he wasn't sure why. He hadn't done anything wrong. He only took the treat the kids left for him. And then he even shared it with the coyote pup.

Mom picked up a handful of snow that contained traces of carrot. Mandy watched, trying to control her anger.

"Did you eat this carrot, Rosco?"

Mom said. Rosco sniffed it.

No. Well, not all of it, he thought. I ate half. Rosco was worried now. He closed his mouth and lowered his head. He looked away from Mom, feeling very sorry. He wished he could tell her he didn't eat the whole thing. He wanted to tell her that he'd given it to the hungry coyote pup that had become separated from his mother.

But no one understood. Mandy scolded him. "Rosco! That was our snowman's nose! You shouldn't have eaten it! What are we going to do now?"

"We'll have to use another rock," said James with a sour look on his face. He removed one of the rocks that was being used as a button and placed it on the snowman's face.

"Oh well, lumpy snowman with holes all over it, plain old rock nose. What does it matter now?" He stepped back to take a look. His shoulders were slumped and he sighed heavily. "Aw, man, it looked so good before."

"It still looks good," said Dad, trying to lighten the mood. "Who needs a carrot nose, after all? Rosco wasn't trying to be bad, kids. He was probably just hungry and curious, as usual. You know how Rosco is. We call him a rascal for a reason…"

He patted Rosco on the head. "It's okay, boy." He turned. "Kids, it was food, after all. We all know how Rosco loves to eat. I guess we just forgot that the nose was *actual* food."

But nothing Dad could say was actually helping. James sighed again. Mandy stomped her foot, still angry.

"He keeps messing up everything that we do out here," she said. "First, my snow angel, then the sticks I found. Now this."

Mom took her phone out of her coat pocket and set it to camera mode.

"It was just a carrot, kids. Don't let this ruin your day. Now, stand next to the snowman, and smile! You'll thank me later for taking this picture." She seemed to have already forgiven Rosco for his mistake.

James and Mandy just shrugged their shoulders. Dad placed the blue hat on the snowman's head.

"Okay, I'm going to get to work," said Dad. "This driveway's not going to shovel itself. You can either let this get you down, or you can move on and forget about it."

The kids each faked a smile. Mom quickly snapped a photo.

"Remember, you wanted to see him play in the snow," she said. "Now that he's here, you've got to be understanding when he doesn't do exactly what you want him to."

"I guess you're right," Mandy said flatly. "But it still makes me mad."

James stared at the ground, still feeling sorry that their masterpiece was wrecked so soon after they had finished it. He stared at Rosco's tracks. But then he noticed something more.

"What's this?" he said, pointing to the ground. "Look how much smaller these tracks are than the others."

Mandy knelt down, suddenly much more curious than upset.

"You're right," she said. "And look. There are two sets of small tracks like the ones I found earlier: one from the woods and one going back into the woods! The puppy! It must've been here!"

Rosco barked a happy sound. They knew! They knew! Yes, the pup was right here! Rosco wished so much that he could explain everything else. But he couldn't. They didn't understand. Or did they?

Mandy stood up and peered into the forest. "That must've been what made the yelping noise that we heard earlier."

"Right. We can try to coax it out of the woods with some dog food," said Dad.

"Okay, that's a good idea. But he's alone in there, with wild animals. Do you think he'll be all right?" she asked doubtfully.

Dad nodded. "I'm sure he'll be all right for a while longer."

"Where do you think his owners are? What if he doesn't come back?"

"Now honey, don't worry. I'm sure he'll be back later," said Mom. "And we'll be here if anyone comes looking for him."

"Okay, okay," Mandy agreed. Then she

turned to her dog. "Rosco, let's go get you a biscuit. You were a bad boy to eat our snowman's nose, but you must be very hungry." Then she turned her back on Rosco with a frown. "Mom, is it almost time for lunch?"

No, they just don't understand, Rosco thought sadly.

CHAPTER 11

LET'S GO SLEDDING

Mandy piled three marshmallows—one on top of the other—to make a tiny snowman on the table. She took a sip of hot cocoa. Everyone had nearly finished eating lunch.

Rosco napped quietly in the corner, sprawled on a blanket on the kitchen floor.

Dad had placed a small pile of Rosco's dog food on the porch for the lost puppy before they'd sat down for the meal.

Mom had brought along her world-famous chili. She had used her own recipe, complete with sour cream, cheddar cheese, and green onions on top, just the way Dad liked it. She'd even brought corn bread to sop up the sauce.

With stomachs full, and fingers warm again, everyone was feeling a lot better. Mandy even started making jokes.

"What do you get when you cross a snowman with a vampire?" she asked.

"Cold teeth?" James answered.

"No. Frostbite!"

Dad groaned. Mom chuckled. James rolled his eyes. He looked out of the window. The sky was a brighter shade of white now, as if the sun were trying to peek through the clouds but couldn't.

"Let's go sledding, Mandy," James said.

"Okay, sure!" Mandy carefully plopped her marshmallow snowman into her mouth.

"I have to go get something upstairs first, though," James continued as he stood up.

"You may be excused from the table," Dad said. "Although you didn't ask," he reminded him.

"Oops, sorry. Thanks Dad." James ran to the loft.

Mom began clearing the table. Mandy took her bowl to the sink.

After the dishes were done, Mandy bundled up once more. Dad went outside and opened the car's trunk. He reached in and pulled out the sleds: a brown toboggan and a bright red saucer sled.

Mom stood with Mandy by the front door. James was still upstairs.

"James, are you almost ready? And where's Rosco?" She glanced outside. "Oh, good, you finished the whole driveway, honey."

"Yeah. That was a lot of work!" Dad said,

yawning. "And now I think I'm ready for an afternoon nap. Mandy, will you mind if I come out with you two later?"

"No, I won't mind, Dad," Mandy said. "I'm sure James won't either."

"I've got Rosco! We're coming!" James called from upstairs.

Mandy fiddled with her mittens, trying to fit her thumbs into the correct holes. Mom straightened Mandy's hat.

Rosco squeezed ahead of James at the top of the skinny spiral staircase.

James was carrying a rope neatly wrapped in circles. It looked like a small lasso.

"What's that for?" Mom asked.

"And why is Rosco wearing his new harness?" Mandy added.

Rosco was indeed wearing his green harness in place of his usual red collar. He looked very sporty. The harness looped down across the front of his chest, behind the tops of each of his front legs, and around his

middle.

"You'll see," James answered with a sly grin, pulling on his snow gear. Mom raised an eyebrow but said nothing.

Rosco discovered the pile of dog food on the porch and began nibbling at it.

"Leave it, Rosco! It's for the puppy!" Mandy reminded him. Rosco obeyed.

CHAPTER 12

FLYING SAUCER

James, Mandy and Dad walked around the cabin to the back yard. A thick, green, snow-covered forest started from behind the cabin and continued into the distance as far as the eye could see. Dad pointed the way to the sledding hill. The rental agency had left directions.

"There it is, the trail that leads to the hill. And look! You can see part of the hill from here!"

It wasn't a very long walk through the snow, and the kids promised to stay on the wide path.

"Be careful now. James, look out for your

sister," said Dad. "Stay out of trouble. And have a good time!"

James and Mandy waved and headed for the trail. Rosco trotted along beside them, excited to go on a walk.

It was tiring but pleasant, hiking in the snowy wilderness. The sharp smell of pine needles mixed with the cold air smelled wonderful.

They had walked only a quarter of a mile when the magnificent white slope rose up beside them. The hill was clear of trees from top to bottom.

"Now that's what I call a sledding hill!" James exclaimed. "Nothing to wreck into!"

"I bet Rosco's going to love this!" Mandy exclaimed. She had forgiven her dog for eating the carrot nose, chewing up the stick arm, and peeing all over the snow angel.

Mandy started up the hill, pulling the saucer sled beside her. James followed with the toboggan. Rosco stayed close behind.

Finally at the top, Mandy sat down on the saucer and faced the bottom of the hill. She huffed and puffed from the steep trek.

"Wow, it looks scary from up here!"

"Nah, it's not scary. We'll be fine," James

71

said, sitting on the toboggan. "Last one down's a rotten egg!" James set his rope in the snow and took off down the hill.

"Okay then, if you say so," Mandy said bravely. She grabbed her rope handles and began leaning from side to side to get the sled to move.

"Here goes nothing!" she cried. In no time at all, she was racing down the hill.

"Wheeeeeee!" she screamed.

At the bottom, they switched sleds each time and hiked back to the top. They rode the hill four more times. The hill was steep and their sleds flew quickly across the snow.

Then, as they climbed back up, James called to his sister as she reached the top of the hill. "Wait! Don't go yet! I want to try something!" He set down the toboggan and hurried over to Mandy.

She had just sat down on the red saucer, ready for her next ride down the hill. He grabbed the strand of rope he'd brought.

"What's that for?" Mandy asked.

He began to unravel it. "I've been working on something. "You'll see."

On one end of the rope, James had secured a metal snap hook, the kind used to attach a leash to a dog collar. He had taken it off of one of Rosco's worn-out collars at home.

"Rosco, come! I have a job for you!" he called.

Rosco bounded over, always willing to help. He had waited at the top of the hill for them each time they'd ridden down, sniffing about as usual, inspecting the area, and always on the lookout for danger.

James fastened the hook to Rosco's harness. Then he took the other end of the rope and tied it to one of the short rope handles on Mandy's saucer. The rope was almost six feet in length.

James checked his knots, and gave a tug on the rope. "Look, he can pull you now, like a sled dog!" he said to Mandy.

"Hmm, are you sure about this, James?

It's a pretty steep hill."

"Well, I've never actually tried it before," James admitted. "But I've researched it, and with Rosco's size and strength, I'm sure he can pull us. It'll be easy for him. That's why he's wearing the harness."

"Maybe we should try this on flat ground first," Mandy cautioned.

Just then, Rosco heard a noise from the trees at the bottom of the hill. What's going on down there?

Rosco wanted to investigate. He pawed at the snow, nervously watching for movement in the forest. He barked.

"What is it Rosco?" Mandy asked, worried now. "What's he barking at, James? Is there something in the trees down there?"

Rosco let out a few short, high-pitched whining noises.

Mandy glanced at James. "What should we do?" But it was too late.

Rosco thought he'd better go see what was there.

In the blink of an eye, Rosco began sprinting downhill, in the direction of the noise. He had completely forgotten that he was attached to a rope.

Mandy had forgotten that the rope on her saucer was attached to Rosco's harness. She had no time to react and no time to get off of her sled.

The rope tugged hard at Mandy's saucer. She grabbed hold of the sled's handles tightly. Like it or not, Mandy was going for a ride!

CHAPTER 13

NO GOING BACK

Rosco loved to race. He loved to chase things. He loved to run. Running downhill with ease was just one of the joys of being a sure-footed, four-legged creature.

But he hadn't counted on the slippery conditions or the steepness of the hill, or the passenger behind him!

Whack! The sled hit Rosco from behind, catching him off guard. He tried to get out of the way, running even faster. But Mandy-on-her-sled flew faster down the hill than any dog could run. In only a few seconds, she slid right into his feet again, going too fast to stop or jump off.

Now Rosco's back legs were sliding under his front legs! He was sliding down the hill *without* a sled!

Mandy panicked and reached for Rosco. But that knocked him over.

He rolled onto his side, still sliding downhill.

Rosco stuck his legs out in front of him

and dug them into the snow, wishing for some brakes! But that didn't work. So he braced himself as he slid—a tangled mess of rope and sled and paws!

"Oh my gosh! Mandy hollered. "Rosco, stop! Can you stop?"

How Rosco wished he could!

Mandy grabbed desperately at the hillside behind and beside her, but it was no use. She could only grab clumps of snow, which broke into powder and slipped through her mittens.

The snow that Rosco kicked up as he toppled down the hill hit Mandy like a hundred miniature snowballs. It stung her eyes and clogged her nose.

The two of them had been traveling with such great speed, that only the flat ground at the bottom of the hill could stop them now.

Finally, Rosco landed at the bottom, dizzy and twisted up in the rope. Mandy smacked into him with a hard thunk.

CHAPTER 14

CARRIED AWAY

James watched in excitement as Mandy and Rosco flew down the hill.

"It's working!" he yelled. "Good job, Rosco!" But he thought Rosco should slow down a little. Then Rosco began to slide.

Uh-oh, Rosco can't stay on his feet.

A couple of seconds later, he watched as Mandy crashed into Rosco at the bottom.

"Oh no!" That wasn't supposed to happen. James felt a sick feeling in his stomach as he jumped on the toboggan, pushed hard against the ground in his mittens, and sped down the hill. In seconds, he arrived at the bottom.

Were they hurt?

"Mandy, Rosco, are you okay? Please be okay!" He had only wanted to make Rosco become a sled dog. Like the ones he saw on TV about the race across Alaska. He never thought anyone might get hurt.

But Rosco and Mandy were lying on the ground like the wreckage of a plane crash.

"Mandy, can you move?"

James knelt down next to her, feeling terribly afraid that his sister might be badly injured.

Mandy looked dazed. She didn't answer.

"Where does it hurt? Did you hit your head?"

"I, I, I think I'm okay," Mandy said. She sat up slowly.

"Oh, thank goodness. I was starting to get really worried! Are you sure?" Mandy nodded. James breathed a sigh of relief.

He turned to Rosco.

"How're you doin', buddy? Are you hurt?" he said, gently running a hand down Rosco's back as he lay there in the snow.

He pulled the rope off of Rosco's ears and from around his neck, where it had become dangerously tangled.

"Come on, Rosco," he whispered. "Please be okay."

The bewildered dog lifted his head.

"Rosco? You're all right? Look, Mandy! He's holding up his head!" Tears filled Mandy's eyes as she nodded with relief.

James dusted the snow off of the dog's snout, and finally, located the latch on his harness, then unhooked it.

Rosco shifted his weight around until he managed to sit up. Then he stood. He shook the snow off of his back and then panted, giving James a half-hearted doggy smile.

Mandy stared at them, still in shock from the wild ride.

"I've never been so scared in my life," she said quietly. "James, I can't believe you did that to me! What were you thinking? You know how fast Rosco can run!" Her voice grew louder as she spoke.

James stood up. He looked straight at the ground. He felt awful.

"I know, I know! I'm so sorry," he begged. "I never thought Rosco would take off like that! I just thought it would be fun if he could pull us on the sled. I thought I was being nice, letting you have the first try."

"Well, it might've been okay if we weren't going downhill," Mandy said. "But no, you really should've gotten on the sled *yourself* the first time, instead of making me your test pilot! I'm not going to trust you *or* your big ideas, anymore, James! You went too far this time! You're just lucky neither of us is really hurt!"

She turned to her dog. "And Rosco! You shouldn't have run off when my sled was attached to you! How could you do that? I'm beginning to think no one around here has any sense at all!"

Rosco made a sorry looking face and looked at the ground. James leaned over to pet the dog's head softly. He certainly hadn't meant for Mandy to get angry with Rosco.

Just then, a shuffling in the trees caught the attention of all three of them. There it is again! Rosco thought. He turned to check his harness. Okay, good. He wasn't attached to that rope anymore. He needed to find out what was going on in there!

Surprised by the sound, the kids forgot their disagreement and turned to listen. The same, high-pitched, yelping noise that they'd heard earlier in the day, came from within the trees. "Ee-oo-ee-oo-ee-oo."

Once again, it sounded like a baby animal, crying out for help. Then came a whimpering sound, but even sadder and more helpless than it had sounded earlier.

Rosco couldn't stop himself. He darted off toward the trees, once again ready to investigate.

"Rosco, wait! Stay here!" Mandy hollered.

But Rosco didn't wait.

"That dog! That dog!" Mandy cried. "He

never listens! Runs off into the trees without giving us a second thought!"

"Shh. I wonder what it is!" James whispered. "It's the same sound from this morning! What if it's that puppy?"

Mandy calmed down and lowered her voice. "Hmm, it could be. It sort of sounded like it. Didn't it?"

"I can't tell for sure. Let's go find out," said James.

"But we're not supposed to go into the forest without Mom or Dad."

"Yeah, but Rosco is with us. Or, *was* with us, and now we have to go get him. And if it *is* the puppy, then it might be hurt. It really sounds like something's wrong, Mandy. We can't just do *nothing*."

At that moment, Rosco gave an alarming bark from inside the forest. "Ruff, ruff, ruff!"

"Rosco!" Mandy called toward the woods. "He sounds far away already, doesn't he? Okay, James, you're right! We have to go! Rosco might be in trouble!"

They left their sleds and headed for the trees. Rosco barked again.

Treading quietly, they walked for a couple of minutes into the tall pine forest, James in front, Mandy close behind. Neither spoke a word.

Suddenly, James stopped walking. Mandy bumped right into him. In front of them stood a large, black, metal cage, about three feet long and two feet high. It looked very out of place in the white wilderness. Rosco stood over the box, wagging his tail wildly and peering down at the creature inside, unsure of what to do. He looked up eagerly as his people approached.

The sad little four-legged animal inside the box was soft and fuzzy, tan and white, with a bushy tail and big, sweet brown eyes.

It *was* the pup.

But it wasn't a regular dog.

"It's a wild animal!" Mandy cried. "And it's trapped in there!"

The pup whined and whimpered some

more. Rosco whimpered back at his newfound friend.

"Mandy, it's a coyote! A coyote puppy! This must be the pup that's been leaving tracks all around our yard!" James exclaimed.

"You're right, James! That wasn't just a lost puppy like I thought! It was a lost *coyote* puppy! And now he's stuck in this awful cage! What are we going to do?

"We've got to get him out. And soon."

"But how? And what is this cage?" Mandy asked. "I've never seen anything like it."

"I think it's called a live trap," James said. "The rangers at the nature center talked about them on our field trip last year. Trappers set them to stop rabbits from destroying their gardens. Or because they want the animal's fur."

"Oh no! But how did he get in there? The cage is closed on all four sides."

"Hmm, let's see. One end of the box should actually be a trap door, I think.

He studied the box.

"Yeah, see, it's right here! And when the trapper sets it, he leaves the trap door open. He'll leave some bait inside the back of the box. Usually it's some sort of food. Then, when an animal comes along and goes into the box, it sets off a trap door. The door goes down and the animal has no time to get out."

"Oh my gosh! Poor thing! He must've

been so hungry that he couldn't resist going after the bait. But he doesn't look hurt. Does he?" Mandy asked.

"No, there's nothing inside that will hurt him. That's why it's called a *live* trap. He's just stuck there, alive, until the trapper comes and checks his traps. But when he does come, that's when this little pup could be in big trouble." James looked very worried. "I'm not sure they'd set him free even though he *is* just a baby."

"Oh my gosh! James, we have to do something! We have to get him out of there!"

"I know! I know!" James fidgeted with the metal walls, looking for an attachment to free the little coyote.

"Be careful, he might bite you," Mandy warned. "He could have rabies."

The pup only whimpered and raised his big, adorable, sad eyes at the two of them.

Rosco watched with concern. He wasn't sure if James knew how to open the trap. And he realized the pup had probably never been so close to humans before—that he must be very scared.

Just as James located the trap door latch, they heard very soft footsteps padding across the snow. The sounds stopped directly behind them. Rosco and the kids turned.

There stood the mother coyote. She let out a fierce growl.

CHAPTER 15

DON'T MOVE

James and Mandy froze. Mandy swallowed hard. The coyote stared at them, revealing her sharp teeth, angry and ready to attack. She stood only a few steps away.

"Don't make any fast moves," James whispered. He slowly moved his hands off of the cage. "It must be the pup's mother. She thinks we did this to him."

Rosco bounded in front of James and Mandy, putting himself between them and the coyote mother. *No one's going to hurt these kids,* he growled.

He would do whatever was necessary to defend Mandy and James, but he understood why she was there. He knew she wanted nothing more than to have her pup back safely, and that she would fight to save him.

They're not going to hurt your pup. They were trying to save him from the trap, he barked and whined. He told her that he'd found her pup and called the people to get him out.

The boy is trying to open the cage, he yipped. *Give him a chance. He can do it. They can save him,* Rosco howled to the coyote. *Just give the boy a chance.*

The coyote understood. She took a long look at James, seeming to think it over. She didn't trust humans. She was a wild animal, and she knew that the safest place for her and her pup was as far away from humans as possible.

Still, she knew there was nothing she could do on her own, to save her baby from the trap.

Slowly, she took a few steps back and stopped growling. But she tilted her ears back and glared hard at the strangers.

Rosco turned to James and then barked in the direction of the trap door. The coyote pup whimpered softly. James understood.

"Rosco wants me to try to open the cage," he whispered to Mandy. Mandy gave him a worried look but nodded.

Gently, James placed his hands on one end of the trap. He fiddled carefully with the steel door. Finally, he found the latch.

"That's it, James," Mandy said softly. "You've got it." He unhooked the latch and slowly lifted the trap door. The pup whined in fear, shrinking back into the farthest corner of the cage.

Rosco trotted over and stuck his nose into the opening of the door.

Come on out, he told the puppy with a few short barks. *They won't hurt you.* The little pup stood up and ran toward the door. In a moment, he was out of the trap. He was free!

He ran to his mother, burying his nose in

her side.   The mother coyote licked her son's back and head. She was overwhelmed with happiness. It had been three whole days since he'd wandered off, three whole days he'd been lost! She thought she might never see him again.

Thank you! She barked to Rosco. She gazed at James and Mandy thankfully for a moment.

Then as quickly and as silently as she had arrived, the mother coyote turned and with the puppy at her side, dashed off into the wilderness. The puppy followed closely, determined not to leave his mother's side again until he was much, much older.

James and Mandy stared as the pair of them disappeared into the distance. They turned and looked at one another in awe.

"Wow! Wow, wow, wow! I can't believe that just happened!" Mandy exclaimed.

"Neither can I!" said James.

"Rosco, that was so brave of you, and so wise! We never should've doubted you. I'm sorry I yelled at you before! And before that and before that!" Mandy said, running her hands over his head and patting him on the back. "You're the best dog ever!" "And James, I'm sorry I got so mad at you, too. It's a good thing you know so much about these kinds of things. I shouldn't have yelled at you for your big ideas before. Your ideas really saved the day this time."

"Aw, it was nothing," James said. "But I'm glad, too!" He laughed. "Otherwise we'd be in big trouble right now!"

CHAPTER 16

NEARLY SPEECHLESS

Back at the cabin, exhausted from a day of adventure, the kids explained what had happened as their parents listened in shock. At first Mom was nearly speechless.

"Don't worry, Mom and Dad," Mandy reasoned. "Because, well, for all the trouble we found today, I guess we should be glad that Rosco runs toward danger, and not away from it. If he hadn't, we might never have known that the coyote pup needed to be rescued. He could've been taken away by the trapper and never would have seen his mother again."

It didn't take long for Mom to gather her

thoughts. "That's true, honey. But you both could have been badly hurt! Rosco, too!"

Yet she figured the kids had acted bravely and done the right thing, however crazy and reckless it sounded to them now.

Dad reacted in a similar way. "Okay, I don't know what else to say about this, kids, except that I'm glad that since Rosco got you *into* trouble, at least he helped get you *out* of trouble. Next time, come get us first, though! Before you go saving any more wild animals! Please!"

Mandy and James nodded and promised they would. Mom placed both hands on her head, sighing loudly. Dad just shook his head back and forth, wishing he had gone sledding with them in the first place. Then all of this trouble might have been prevented. Or at least he could've been there to help.

CHAPTER 17

SNOWBALL FIGHT

The next morning, after breakfast, Mom was cleaning up the kitchen.

"Daddy! James! Where are you guys?" Mandy called as she stepped out onto the porch, finally dressed and ready for the snow. She couldn't find her brother or her father anywhere. "Mom, do you know where they went?"

"Outside, I think," Mom answered.

But there was no rustling in the bushes, no snow falling from the tree branches, not even any wind blowing. And there was no sign of James or Dad.

Whack! A snowball hit Mandy in the

stomach. Whack, again! A third snowball hit the cabin wall next to the front door. A fourth one hit her in the leg. Surprised, she ran down the porch stairs and found safety behind a tall tree trunk.

"Man! You guys really know how to gang up on someone!" she called.

James was hiding behind the snowman in the yard. Dad was hiding behind the minivan. Four more speedy snowballs came flying by Mandy's head.

"Missed me! But, okay, that does it! I'm going to get you guys!" Mandy hollered.

"Come on, Mom! It's time for a snowball fight! Time to get 'em!" she yelled, as loudly as she could.

Mandy scooped up some snow. She began to throw snowballs in the direction of her dad and brother. Soon the two of them came out from their hiding spots, and they all hurled snowballs at each other in the open yard.

A minute later, Mom quietly opened the

front door and cautiously crept outside in her snow gear and boots. She knelt down to pick up some snow, patted it into a nice, round snowball. She crouched down so she wouldn't be noticed.

Just then, Rosco came barreling out, pushing the door open wide in front of him. It slammed shut with a loud bang. He raced down the stairs, slipping and sliding to the bottom.

Everyone froze and turned to watch. They all spotted Mom. Immediately, Mom fell under heavy fire. Mom dodged two snowballs. The third one hit her in the arm.

"Look out! Here I come!" she called and raced down the stairs, almost falling off the bottom step.

Meanwhile, Rosco wagged his tail at them and hunched down into his *let's-play* position in the yard. But he wasn't sure what game they were all playing.

James threw a snowball at Rosco. The snowball was headed straight for his face! But this game was nothing new to Rosco. He loved to catch tennis balls that the kids would throw to him, and he was good at it. He jumped up and caught the snowball mid-air, without a second thought. He swallowed it like a treat.

"Oh, my gosh! You're amazing, Rosco!" James stopped to throw him another and another. He jumped and caught them all, then ate them all.

Everyone laughed and cheered.

"Now that's quite a trick!" Mom exclaimed. "Maybe Rosco belongs in the circus! Or on a baseball team!"

Just then, a loud howling sound came from far off in the forest.

They all stopped to listen. But this howl didn't sound threatening. It just sounded like nature at its finest.

"Ow-ow-ow-ooooooooooooooo!"

"I'll bet it's the mother coyote!" James said. They waited, wondering if she'd howl again.

A few seconds later, they heard another howl. But this one sounded like a much younger coyote had made the noise. The howl was broken and cute, and was followed by a few excited high-pitched yelps.

"That's the little coyote, the puppy!" Mandy cried. "I'll bet they're saying hello or maybe goodbye! Or that they're doing fine out there? That they're happy to be free!"

Rosco could not help but answer this call from the wild. "Ar-oooooo!" he called. "Ar-oooooo! Ar-oooooo!" Then he barked.

James picked up another clump of snow and began packing it into a snowball. "Who's ready for another snowball fight?" he asked.

"I am!" Mandy called.

He threw it. The snowball sailed across the yard. Mandy ducked, just in the nick of time.

About The Author

Shana Gorian, originally from western Pennsylvania, lives in Southern California with her husband and two children, and the real *Rosco*, their German shepherd. She and her family visit the mountains every winter in search of the perfect sledding hill.

Note: Never approach animals in the wild! They can be very dangerous. This is a story of fiction and children should always stay away from wild animals.

Ros Webb is an artist based in Ireland. She has produced a multitude of work for books, digital books and websites. Samples of her art can be seen on Facebook: Ros Webb Book Illustration.

Josh Addessi is a quirky illustrator and animation professor based in Northwest Indiana. He has digitally painted all manner of book covers, stage backdrops and trading cards. Samples of his art can be seen at http://joshaddessi.blogspot.com/

Tori March is an illustrator and 3D sculptor. She aided in painting this book cover. Samples of her art can be seen at https://www.artstation.com/artist/victoriamarch

The *real* Rosco is every bit as loveable and rascally as the fictional Rosco. He loves to catch snowballs in his mouth, too.

Visit **shanagorian.com** to sign up for her email list. And be sure to join Rosco the Rascal for more adventures in the series!

Made in United States
Troutdale, OR
12/16/2023

15955081R00067